The Jolly Steamship

by Harry Rowohlt * illustrated by Walter Trier

North
South

First published in the United States, Great Britain, Canada, Australia, and New Zealand in 2013
by NorthSouth Books Inc., an imprint of NordSüd Verlag AG, CH-8005 Zürich, Switzerland.

Distributed in the United States by NorthSouth Books Inc., New York 10016.
Library of Congress Cataloging-in-Publication Data is available.
Printed in Germany by Grafisches Centrum Cuno GmbH & Co. KG, 39240 Calbe, January 2013.
ISBN: 978-0-7358-4127-7
1 3 5 7 9 • 10 8 6 4 2
www.northsouth.com

*

"We're ready to sail! All aboard if you please!"
But that doesn't please the Pekingese.

*

"Three clever dolphins! Look over there!"
The Pekingese just doesn't care.

✳

＊

"The world's biggest mammal's the wonderful whale."
The Peke doesn't even wag its tail.

＊

*

"What a sensation! A flying fish!"
"I wish," says the Peke, "he'd fly into my dish!"

*

*

The swordfish has made a kebab on its spike.
"You can make a kebab with whatever you like."

*

The sea horse says, "Here's my bit of the sea,
But you're welcome to share my algae with me."

*

The nice seal family smiles a lot.
"Never complain, and enjoy what you've got."

*

"My funny fur seal face feels fine
'Cos this fellow's face is funnier than mine."

✳

"There are plenty of tasty fish in the sea,"
Says the turtle, "so why is he fishing for me?"

✳

*

"I'm a dishy jellyfishy.
Call me squishy if you wishy."

*

✳

This is a sight you'll never forget:
The octopus playing a jazz quartet.

✳

The clouds are dancing overhead,
But the weary sun looks ready for bed.

✳

Even the Peke wants to sail next year.

"Things come and go, but the sea stays here."

*